In Memory of Len[i]
For Calvin - you have mad[e]
~G.H.

NightinGail Books

www.NightinGailBooks.com

A BIG thank you to my husband and family for being patient with me as I work through my creative process.
~J.K.

WHITE FOX
Art & Design

www.WhiteFoxAD.com

More Alike Than Different...A Down Syndrome Awareness Tale
by Gail Hamblin

Copywrite 2017 by Gail Hamblin. All rights reserved.
No part of this book may be reproduced in any written, electronic, recording, or photocopying form without written permission of the author Gail Hamblin, or illustrator Jenny Cherriman Kopp. Reproduction for an entire school or district is prohibited. Books may be purchased in quantity and/or special sales by contacting the author, Gail Hamblin by email at gail@nightingailbooks.com.

Library of Congress Control Number:
ISBN-13:
978-0692856789 (NightinGail Books)
ISBN-10: 0692856781

First Edition

My name is Arthur and I have Down Syndrome.

That night
as I brushed my teeth,
I looked deeply
into the mirror.

Am I really so different?

"What are you doing?"
my sister, Alissa asked.

"I am sad because
I am different,"
I replied.

"Arthur, we are all different," she said.

"I have seen you on the swings, I like those too. Do you see? I am just like you," she explained.

splashing in the pool, and playing ball.

Now I am happy because I know for sure that...

Seth was wrong!

Alissa's words were true.

I am more alike than different!

Clyde said, "Sure!"

"Are you going to play with me too?" I asked.

I thought about what to say to Seth next.

I said, "Hey Seth, we are more alike than different. I like pizza, music, and games. Do you like those too?"

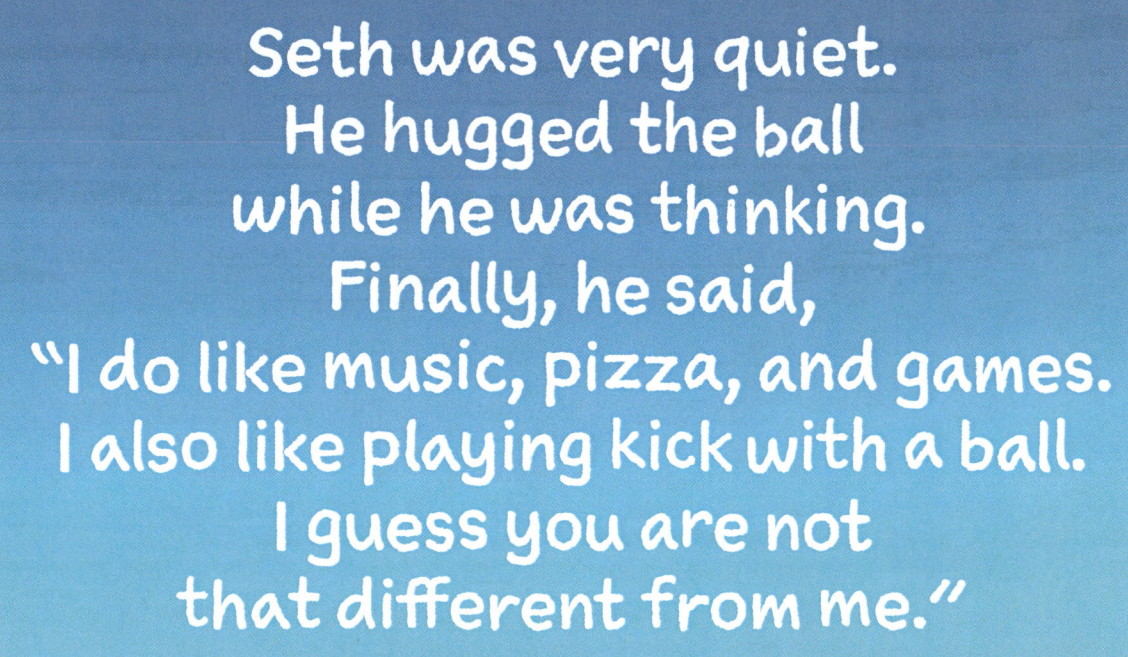

Seth was very quiet.
He hugged the ball
while he was thinking.
Finally, he said,
"I do like music, pizza, and games.
I also like playing kick with a ball.
I guess you are not
that different from me."

Seth decided it was okay to play with me too. So, all three of us played with the ball together.

Being together with them felt splendid.

Questions for the Author

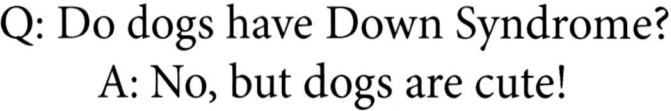

Q: Do dogs have Down Syndrome?
A: No, but dogs are cute!

Q: Do people with Down Syndrome really have bigger tongues?
A: Sometimes! Some people with Down Syndrome have bigger tongues. Also, some people have smaller jaws which makes their tongue look like it is bigger.

Q: Are people with Down Syndrome shorter than other people?
A: Sometimes! Usually babies that are born with Down Syndrome grow at a slower rate than other babies. Doctors use a special growth chart just for kids and babies with Down Syndrome. Adults with Down Syndrome can be shorter than other people. But, they can also be taller.

Q: Do people with Down Syndrome like the same things I like?
A: There is one way to know for sure! Find a person who has Down Syndrome and ask them!

How do I make friends with a person with Down Syndrome?

I understand! It can be scary to make new friends. But, making friends with someone with Down Syndrome is very similar to making friends with anyone else. Here are some tips to help you start.

1. **Smile** - The first thing a new friend sees is your beautiful smile!

2. **Say Hello or Wave** - Let the person know you want to talk.

3. **Compliment Them** - Are they wearing a nice shirt? Do they have cool looking sunglasses? Is their backpack your favorite color? Find something you like and say something nice.

4. **Listen** - If the person talks, uses sign language, or gives you a smile back, listen. The person is trying to get to know you too.

5. **Play** - Nothing says we are friends more than playing together!

6. **Ask Questions** - Finding out what you both like is as easy as asking questions. Start with things you like. You will love finding out how much you have in common.
Try these: Do you like ice cream?
Do you like to swim?
What is your favorite movie?
We are ALL more ALIKE than different!

Down Syndrome Facts

~Down Syndrome is not a disease. It is a chromosomal condition. Down Syndrome occurs when an extra 21st chromosome is present ("What is Down Syndrome?", 2016).

~ There are three types of Down Syndrome. They are: Mosaic, Translocation, and Trisomy 21 ("What is Down Syndrome?", 2016).

~ There is a greater number of individuals living with Trisomy 21 than with Mosaic Down Syndrome and Translocation ("What is Down Syndrome?", 2016).

~ 1 in every 792 liveborn babies has Down Syndrome (De Graaf, Buckley, Skotko, 2016).

Reference List

De Graaf G., Buckley F., Skotko B. (2016). Estimation of the number of people with Down syndrome in the United States. Genetics in Medicine.

What Is Down Syndrome? (2016, October 6) Retrieved from http://www.ndss.org/Down-Syndrome/What-Is-Down-Syndrome/

Resources for Parents & Teachers:

National Down Syndrome Congress
https://www.ndsccenter.org/education/
Toll Free: 1-800-232-NDSC (6372)
Email: info@ndsccenter.org

National Down Syndrome Society
http://www.ndss.org/
Helpline 1-800-221-4602
Email: info@ndss.org

Down Syndrome Education USA
https://www.dseusa.org/en-us/

Down Syndrome Awareness:
~More Alike Awareness Campaign
~ March 21st each year is observed as World Down Syndrome Day. https://worlddownsyndromeday.org/
~ Rock Your Socks is a movement for people to spread Down Syndrome Awareness by wearing crazy, unmatched socks to celebrate World Down Syndrome Day on March 21st every year.

Made in the USA
Coppell, TX
13 March 2025

47049861R00021